BAILEY AND FRIENDS

BY: LISA KIICK

Illustrator: Ryan Stouch

First Edition: Three Short Illustrated Stories for Young Children

First published by Dog Ear Publishing
4010 W. 86th Street, Ste H
Indianapolis, IN 46268
www.dogearpublishing.net

ISBN: 978-159858-743-2

Printed in the United States of America

Table of Contents

Bailey's New Friends

It was a warm spring morning and Bailey was just getting out of bed. She looked around the bedroom and saw that Mom and Dad's bed was made. She thought, "Gee they're already up."

Not wanting to miss anything, Bailey ran downstairs to the kitchen where she found Mom who when she saw Bailey, leaned down to pet her and give her a kiss on the head. Bailey wagged her tail happily.

Bailey, a toy American Eskimo, is a cream colored furry little dog with big brown eyes, pointy ears, long white eyelashes, and a black button nose, knew she was cute. Her Mom and Dad had told her this many times.

Mom quickly gave Bailey her biscuit and Cheerios and watched her gobble them up. Mom and Dad always shared their favorite cereal with her in the morning.

Bailey walked out to the screened in porch and went outside through the little door her Dad had made which made it easy for Bailey to go out to the yard whenever she wanted.

As she went outside, Mom said, "Make sure you stay in our yard Bailey." Bailey always did. She knew she was never to leave the yard.

Bailey walked over to her favorite spot and laid down. She loved lying in the sun and liked watching all the little animals at her Dad's feeders. He fed them corn and bird seed everyday.

Bailey often wished she had a little friend to play with, but her Mom and Dad had told her many times where they lived they were allowed only one pet. Mom would say to Bailey, "Someday we will have our own house and then you can have some playmates."

Bailey always thought, "Gee, wonder when that will be? Oh well, I'll just have to wait."

Bailey looked over at the feeders, watching a little chipmunk eating corn. All of a sudden out of the corner of her eye she saw that nasty black cat from next door cross their yard. The cat grabbed the poor little chipmunk and she was screaming and kicking her little legs.

Bailey jumped up and ran, yelling at the cat. "Let go of that chipmunk, you are going to hurt it!" The cat was so surprised that it dropped the chipmunk and ran off.

Walking slowly toward the chipmunk Bailey was afraid it was hurt or worse. To her surprise the chipmunk jumped up and exclaimed, "Oh my goodness, you saved my life. Thank-you, Thank-you!"

Looking worried Bailey asked the chipmunk, "Are you ok?"

The little chipmunk smiled saying, "Yes yes, thanks!"

Lifting her paw Bailey brushed the dirt off the chipmunk's back. They sat and talked to each other a little and the whole time

Bailey kept thinking, "Gee, she's really nice, someone to play with!"

Bailey looking over at the feeders, saw something move and thought maybe the cat was back, but it was a baby squirrel. She had never seen a squirrel that small. Bailey started to walk toward the baby squirrel and she could see it was shaking.

She thought, "The poor little squirrel probably saw the cat trying to hurt the chipmunk."

"Hi, are you alright?" Bailey asked quietly as she sat down. The baby squirrel started walking slowly toward Bailey and the chipmunk. Bailey softly said, "It's ok, the cat is gone. I scared him and he ran away."

The baby squirrel, still shaking, asked, "Are you sure? I was so afraid!"

Bailey could see tears running down the baby squirrel's cheeks. Smiling she said, "Don't worry, you are safe. Come over and talk to us." The baby squirrel joined Bailey and the chipmunk.

Bailey looking at them smiled and said, "My name is Bailey and I live in this house with my Mom and Dad."

The baby squirrel and the chipmunk looked at each other. Bailey asked, "What are your names?"

"We don't have any names," they answered.

Bailey thought for a minute and said, "Well I will give you each a name!"

The chipmunk jumped up and down exclaiming, "Me first, me first!"

Bailey looked at her and said, "Gee, you're really pretty with your light brown fur and those beautiful black and white marks down your back. I'm going to name you 'Gabby'!"

The chipmunk jumped up and down again, smiled and said, "Oh, that's a beautiful name. I love it!"

Laughing, Bailey said, "Gee you're really a happy little chipmunk."

The baby squirrel was standing up looking at Bailey and said quietly, "What's my name?"

Bailey stood back and said, "Well you have a beautiful snow white belly and shiny gray fur, and I love your long furry tail. I think I'll name you 'Betsy'!"

Betsy sat there smiling looking up at Bailey who smiled back and said, "Boy you're really bashful."

Both of them giggling said, "Oh Bailey we love our names, thank you!"

Bailey happily said, "We can all be best friends!"

Gabby and Betsy were grinning from ear to ear and said, "We never had a friend."

Patting them on the head, Bailey said, "I'm glad you're my friends. We can have great fun together."

Just then, Bailey's Mom called out the window that it was time to come in and eat. Bailey turned to her new friends and said, "That's my Mom. I have to go now, but I'll see you tomorrow."

Gabby and Betsy said, "Goodbye," and waved as they ran off.

Bailey sat there a minute looking around, and thought, "Good the cat was no where in sight."

Bailey ran in the house and her Mom said, "Dad will be home soon for dinner, but it's time for you to eat."

Later that night when Bailey got into bed, Mom and Dad kissed her good night and told her how much they loved her.

Bailey knew how lucky she was to have them, and as she closed her eyes to go to sleep she grinned and thought, "I can't wait until tomorrow to see my two new friends and playmates, Gabby and Betsy!"

Gabby and Betsy's Homes

Bailey crawled out of bed and stretched her little legs, all four of them.

She sat there a minute and thought, "Oh Mom and Dad have to go to work today, they must be downstairs."

Bailey flew down the stairs as fast as she could go and into the kitchen. Mom and Dad both said, "Good morning Bailey did you sleep well?" Bailey wagged her tail and barked. Mom smiled asking, "Are you ready for your biscuit and Cheerios?" Bailey started running around in a circle and Mom dropped them on the floor.

It did not take Bailey long to finish them. She was very hungry and excited about going outside to see her new friends, Gabby and Betsy. She hoped they were ok and had no problem with the neighbor's cat.

Mom and Dad kissed Bailey on the head and said, "We have to go to work now. You be a good girl, and when you go outside remember to stay in our yard."

Bailey watched them go out the door. When she heard the car leave, she dashed out to the porch and ran through her little door to the yard. Bailey stopped quickly when she saw the nasty cat in the yard.

The cat looked at Bailey, thinking, "So what are you going to do now?"

Bailey stared at the cat and started running and barking. The cat took off down the alley and around the corner. "Good, Bailey thought, I'll show him, he's not going to pick on my little friends."

Bailey turned around to go back toward her house when she saw Gabby and Betsy. Bailey waved and said, "Hi, I wondered where you were!"

Gabby stretched and yawned and said, "Betsy and I just woke up when we saw you chasing that cat."

Grinning, Bailey said, "No problem I just showed him who's boss in my yard."

Bailey walked closer to her friends and looked at both of them and said, "Gabby, you have ground all over your head and back," as she brushed it off with her paw, "how did you get so dirty?"

"I just got out of bed," answered Gabby.

Curious, Bailey asked, "Gee where do you live?"

"Come on I'll show you," Gabby offered.

Bailey and Betsy followed Gabby around the corner of the house to where some bushes were planted. Gabby stopped, turned around looking very proud of herself, and pointed to a little hole in the ground between the bushes.

"This is where I live," Gabby said.

Bailey and Betsy staring at the hole looked at each other and asked, "You live in the ground?"

Gabby shook her head up and down and said, "Yes, it's very nice and warm. I keep corn down there too. It's a long tunnel and I sleep in there at night."

Trying to hide their disbelief, Bailey and Betsy could not imagine living under the ground, Bailey said, "I bet it's really nice. Too bad we can't see it, but the hole is too small for us to go down."

Gabby signed and said, "Yeah, it's real nice. I wish you could see it too."

Betsy leaned over and tapped Bailey on her leg. Looking up at her she asked sadly, "Don't you and Gabby want to see where I live?"

Bailey and Gabby happily said, "Oh, yes we do!"

Turning, Betsy smiled and said, "Just follow me!"

Betsy ran toward the back yard to a large pine tree with lots of pine needles and pine cones laying around. She jumped up on the trunk of the tree and crawled slowly to her nest. It was made of small sticks, grass, pine needles and leaves.

She turned around and exclaimed, "This is where I live and sleep, and when I get better at climbing, I'll build a nest higher up in the tree."

Just then Betsy screamed! She lost her balance and fell out of her nest.

Luckily, Bailey ran under the tree hoping to catch her. Betsy fell on Bailey's back and slid down her tail onto the ground.

Betsy started crying and said, "Boy, I feel really stupid. Thanks Bailey, you saved me."

Gabby and Bailey checked to make sure she was alright. Poor Betsy looked so upset and embarrassed.

Bailey softly said, "Don't worry Betsy, you'll get better at climbing when you get bigger. Remember you're still a little baby. Gabby and I will help take care of you."

Betsy wiped her tears and looked at both of them and smiled.

Bailey walked over to lay in the sun and watched Gabby and Betsy run over to eat corn at her Dad's feeders. Looking down the alley, Bailey saw Mom and Dad in their car coming home from work. She thought, "Boy the day went fast!"

Bailey ran over to her friends and said, "I have to go in soon. I just saw Mom and Dad pull in the garage."

Gabby looked at Bailey and asked, "Betsy and I were wondering if maybe tomorrow we can come and see where you live?"

Bailey sat there thinking for a few seconds and said, "Well, sure, but we have to wait until Mom and Dad go to work, so I don't get in trouble."

Betsy and Gabby both smiling said, "Great we'll see you tomorrow!" They said, "Goodnight," as Bailey ran in the house waiting to greet Mom and Dad.

After dinner, when it was time to go to bed, Mom and Dad kissed Bailey good night and said, "You're a good little girl and we love you very much!" Bailey wagged her tail and looked at both of them thinking to herself, "I sure hope everything goes well tomorrow when Gabby and Betsy visit our house." Bailey closed her eyes and sighed thinking about tomorrow's visit.

Visiting Bailey's House

The sun was shining through the bedroom window. Bailey opened her eyes and laid there for a few seconds. She thought, "Boy my belly really hurts."

She crawled out of bed and just sat there. Bailey was wondering why her belly hurt so bad. Then she remembered, "Oh, yea, Gabby and Betsy are coming to visit my house."

Bailey was so upset. She was afraid something might go wrong when Mom and Dad were at work. She thought, "Oh well, I will keep things under control, at least I hope I will."

Walking slowly down the steps Bailey saw her Mom and Dad eating breakfast at the table. Dad looked down at her and said, "Hi, Bailey, we wondered when you were going to crawl out of bed."

Mom said, "I'll get your biscuit and Cheerios." She went to the cupboard, came back to the table and laid Bailey's treats on the floor.

Bailey just sniffed them and walked away. Dad leaned over and picked her up. Petting and hugging her, he said, "Bailey what's wrong?" Does your belly hurt?" Bailey just looked up at him with her big sad eyes.

Mom leaned over and kissed Bailey on the cheek. She whispered to Dad, "Maybe she should go outside, she'll probably just eat some grass, that always makes her belly feel better."

Dad put her down on the floor and said, "Ok you can go outside and we'll check on you before we go to work."

Bailey went out to the porch and through her little door to the
yard. She walked around sniffing and started eating some grass.

Gabby and Betsy were at the feeders eating and yelled, "Hi,
Bailey." Bailey just looked up sadly and said nothing.

They looked at each other and Betsy asked, "What's wrong with Bailey?"

Gabby said, "Let's go ask her."

They ran over to Bailey and both said, "What's wrong Bailey, and why are you eating grass?"

Bailey looked up and said, "My belly hurts a little and eating grass makes it feel better."

They both said sadly, "Oh, we're sorry you feel bad."

Bailey loved her little friends and didn't want them to know she was worried about them coming to visit her house.

Bailey saw Mom and Dad coming out of the house and ran over to them wagging her tail. Mom smiled and leaned down rubbing Bailey's little belly and said, "Are you feeling better? You look better. You be a good girl today and we'll see you after work." Bailey watched them walk to the garage and leave for work.

Gabby and Betsy were sitting at the feeder watching all of this. Gabby said sadly to Betsy, "Gee wish we had a Mom and Dad like Bailey does."

Betsy agreed, "Yeah, that would be nice, but we have a great friend, Bailey!"

Bailey ran over to join her little friends. Gabby was concerned and said, "Are you feeling better?"

"Yes, much better, thanks," Bailey answered.

Betsy looked up smiling at Bailey and asked, "Can we go see your house now?"

Smiling, Bailey said, "Yes, but first there are three rules I need to tell you before we go in. These are Mom and Dad's rules made for me."

Betsy and Gabby both said excitedly, "Ok, what are they?"

Bailey said, "The first rule is you cannot go to the bathroom on the floor."

Gabby and Betsy looked at each other and giggled. Gabby whispered, "We both went a little while ago."

"Good, and the second rule is you can't get on the furniture," Bailey said.

"What's that?" Betsy asked.

Bailey said, "Well, oh, you'll see it when we go inside. The third rule is, we can't knock anything over!"

Gabby and Betsy, shaking their heads up and down, promised Bailey they would be good and follow the three rules! Bailey thought, "Boy, I sure hope so!"

All three of them ran over to the porch and through the little door into the kitchen.

Gabby stopped and exclaimed, "Wow this is a big place!"

Betsy looked around and said, "Yeah, it's kind of scary!" Gabby shook her head agreeing with Betsy.

Bailey smiled and said, "Let me show you the other rooms." They walked into the living room and Bailey said, "This is the furniture that we are not allowed to sit on."

Betsy stared and said, "Boy, it sure looks soft. Can I just touch it?"

Bailey said, "Sure, but be careful, don't scratch it."

Betsy walked over and put her tiny paw on it and exclaimed, "Oh wow that's really soft!"

"Yeah, too bad I can't sleep on it," Bailey said as she walked over to a large wicker basket that was full of stuffed toys.

"These are my toys that I play with. Sometimes Dad and I play with them together," Bailey said proudly.

Gabby and Betsy looked at them in amazement and said, "Gee, we don't have any toys!"

"Well the next time you visit we can play with all of them," Bailey promised.

"Gabby looked around and asked, "What's that noise I hear?"

Bailey said, "Oh that's a radio. Mom and Dad leave it on so I don't get lonely. Sometimes I dance to the music."

"What's dance?" Gabby asked.

"I'll show you," Bailey said, as she stood up on her back legs and started dancing around and moving her front paws to the music.

Gabby and Betsy started laughing. Betsy said excitedly, "I'm going to try that!"

"Me, too!" yelled Gabby.

All three were standing on their back legs dancing. Betsy was really good, she did a flip in the air and landed on her feet. Bailey and Gabby stared, they couldn't believe it. Gabby started rolling around on her back, kicking her little feet in the air. They were all laughing and having a great time.

Bailey stopped, her little tongue was hanging out of her mouth. Out of breath she said, "Gee, we've been dancing a long time. I'm tired and thirsty, would you like some water?"

They both answered, "Yes, please!" They walked over to Bailey's water dish and each had a drink.

Bailey laid down and said, "I'm really tired after all that dancing." Gabby and Betsy joined Bailey and snuggled up against her warm belly and they all went to sleep.

Sometime later, Bailey woke up and wondered how long they had been sleeping. Gabby and Betsy were still sound asleep.

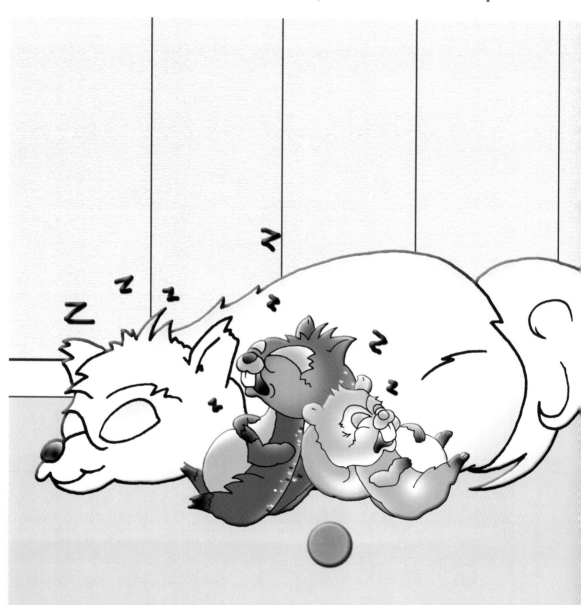

Bailey suddenly jumped up, as she heard the porch door open. "Oh no, Mom and Dad are home!" exclaimed Bailey.

Gabby and Betsy jumped straight up in the air. They were shaking and scared. They looked at Bailey and screamed, "What should we do, Bailey?"

Bailey pointed, exclaiming, "Quick, run over behind that table and hide! I'll distract them when they come in and you sneak out through the porch."

Betsy and Gabby raced over to the table and hid.

Mom and Dad walked in the room and Mom called out, "Bailey where are you?"

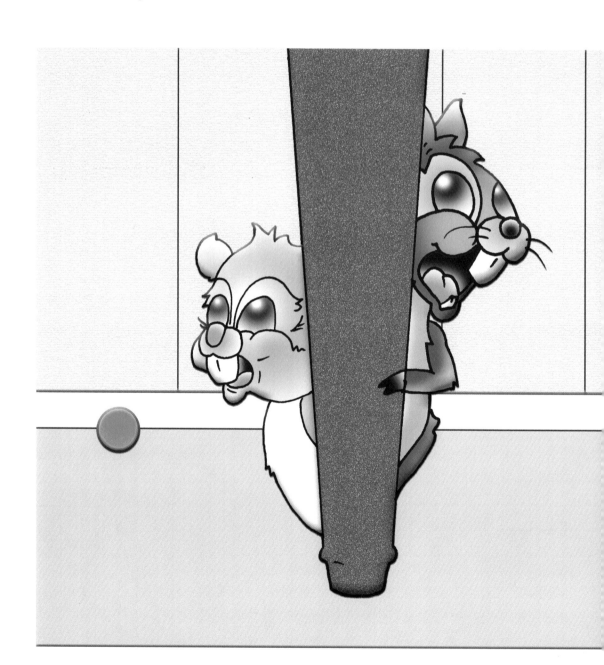

Bailey ran by the table where Gabby and Betsy were hiding and whispered, "Sneak out when they're not looking and I'll see you tomorrow."

Mom picked up Bailey, who was so excited to see her parents. They both kissed her and Dad said, "Well Bailey you're excited. You must be feeling better!"

Bailey just kept licking their faces. As she looked down she saw Gabby and Betsy run through the kitchen and out the little door on the porch.

That night when Bailey crawled into bed, she thought, "Boy I sure am tired."

Mom and Dad kissed her good night and her little eyes were already closed. Bailey thought, "Gee, that was a close one today, but I had the greatest time with my little friends. Wonder what we'll do tomorrow?"

Lisa Kiick and Bailey

Printed in the United States
130207LV00003B